This story is based on the ICARUS project, which has been carried out at the foot of Mount Etna in Sicily since 2011. A family in that area, the Rostas, cooperated closely with Prof. Dr. Martin Wikelski, Director at the Max Planck Institute of Animal Behavior in Radolfzell, Germany.

My special thanks go to the families of Benito and Giuseppe Rosta and their beautiful and sensitive Sicilian goats. Without their support, the project on Mount Etna, and this story, would not have happened. A big thank you goes to Enzo Spartà from Etna Quota Mille in Randazzo. It all started when he connected us with the local community. He still supports our work today.

I dedicate this book to Larissa, Laura, Fiona, and Martin. —U.M.

For Luna and for all of the wonderful animals and their many astounding, mysterious talents. —B.L.

Text copyright © 2024 by Uschi Müller
Illustrations copyright © 2024 by Brittany Ferguson

24 25 26 27 28 5 4 3 2 1

Greystone Kids / Greystone Books Ltd.
greystonebooks.com

Cataloguing data available from Library and Archives Canada
ISBN 978-1-77164-928-5 (cloth)
ISBN 978-1-77164-929-2 (epub)

Editing by Kallie George, Tiffany Stone, and Jane Billinghurst
Copy editing by Becky Noelle
Proofreading by Tanya Trafford
Cover and interior design by Sara Gillingham Studio

Printed and bound in China on FSC®-certified paper at Shenzhen Reliance Printing. The FSC® label means that materials used for the product have been responsibly sourced.

Greystone Books thanks the Canada Council for the Arts, the British Columbia Arts Council, the Province of British Columbia through the Book Publishing Tax Credit, and the Government of Canada for supporting our publishing activities.

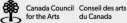

Canadä

BRITISH COLUMBIA | BRITISH COLUMBIA ARTS COUNCIL
An agency of the Province of British Columbia

Canada Council Conseil des arts
for the Arts du Canada

FSC
MIX
Paper from responsible sources
www.fsc.org FSC® C102842

Greystone Books gratefully acknowledges the xʷməθkʷəy̓əm (Musqueam), Sḵwx̱wú7mesh (Squamish), and səl̓ilwətaɬ (Tsleil-Waututh) peoples on whose land our Vancouver head office is located.

Salvatore and the Goats of Mount Etna

BY USCHI MÜLLER • ILLUSTRATIONS BY BRITTANY LANE

DAVID SUZUKI INSTITUTE

GREYSTONE KIDS

GREYSTONE BOOKS • VANCOUVER / BERKELEY / LONDON

At the foot of white-peaked Mount Etna lay a little goat farm. Etna was an active volcano. It often rumbled, and sometimes even spewed lava. But the farm was on the north side, where it was safe and the soil was rich. So, Salvatore and his parents made their home there, with their herding dog, Gina.

And, of course,
the goats.

Salvatore loved the goats very much.
They were curious, constantly checking out what was going on

around,

and even *behind*, them.

Bianca, the lead goat, was Salvatore's favorite. When she leaned her soft nose against his face, it felt like she was sharing secrets with him. "Goats don't share secrets," said his papa gruffly.

But Salvatore wasn't so sure.

Bianca seemed to know more about the mountain than he did.

Today, Salvatore was going to take the goats to graze high up on the mountain, the best place for tasty herbs and fresh spring water. Salvatore had always gone with his papa before. This morning he was going all by himself.

He was excited
and only a little nervous.

His mamma gave him some food and water. His papa gave him some advice. "Don't let those goats boss you around. Remember, YOU herd the goats. They don't herd you."

"Yes, Papa," said Salvatore. "I'll be back before sunset."

And, with a whistle to Gina, off he went.

Salvatore, Gina, and the goats climbed higher and higher. Usually, Bianca helped lead the way.

But today, she circled Salvatore.

"Are you looking out for me on my first day alone?"
He smiled and gave her head a scratch.

"Don't worry. It's my job to look after you."

At last, they reached the perfect spot, near the top, and the goats began to pick at the grass. It was beautiful on the mountain, although a little quiet. Usually there were birds singing. But today, the meadows were hushed.

Maybe the birds were off picnicking on berries.
The thought made Salvatore want a snack too.

But no sooner had Salvatore reached into his pack
than Bianca began to kick and jump around.

"Bianca, calm down," said Salvatore.
But Bianca did not.

Then another goat began to kick! And another!

Salvatore looked around. He didn't see any danger.

Even so, soon ALL the goats were tossing their heads and kicking their hooves.

Gina began barking.

Salvatore tried to get close to Bianca. But she was too wild.
"Gina! Quick! Help!" cried Salvatore.

Too late! Bianca took off, back down the mountain.
The other goats fled after her. Gina and Salvatore sped after them.
Salvatore's heart raced. "Stop! Stop!" he cried.

His papa had said, "Don't let the goats herd you!"
And now, that was exactly what was happening!

"Bianca! Stop!" he cried once more.

For a fleeting moment, Bianca turned to him.
Her eyes were wild with panic.

Salvatore knew what his father had said.
Yet, instead of running ahead and forcing the goats
to stop, he let them go.

Something was wrong.

He *had* to trust them.

But his fear grew as the goats headed toward
a little birch wood at the bottom of the mountain.
It was the spot where wild dogs often lay in wait.

To his alarm, Bianca and the others
slowed and gathered there.

Salvatore was completely out of breath when
he finally caught up with them.

"There, there," said Salvatore, trying to sound calm. He stroked Bianca's soft nose. "We must get out of here, in case any wild dogs are near." The fur on Gina's back stood up straight. "Papa will be so mad at me if anything happens to the goats," thought Salvatore.

But before he could try to move them, there was a loud rumbling overhead.

It wasn't the rumble of a wild dog. It was much louder—much more frightening. It was the mountain itself. The mountain was roaring! Salvatore's eyes went wide. "*Oh no,*" he whispered.

All at once, Salvatore knew what the goats were running from! They were running from the mountain. But how had they known?

The goats were huddled together and trembling. "I have to get them home," thought Salvatore. "We'll be safe there."

He took off his scarf and approached Bianca.
"You are such a good leader," he said softly.
"The other goats trust you. I need your help."
Bianca listened. Gently, Salvatore reached out
and tied his scarf around her neck.

He led her to a little-used trail, the fastest way back to
the farm. It was narrow, and the other goats were wary
at first but began to follow.

Slowly, they descended into the valley.

Gina ran behind the herd to
make sure no goat was forgotten.

When they returned to the farmyard, Mamma, Papa, and the whole family were waiting. Mamma and Papa had tears in their eyes. "You're safe!"

Salvatore explained what had happened. Papa listened gravely.

"Oh, Salvatore," said Papa. "You did exactly right. You, and the goats. This time, I am glad you let them lead."

Salvatore hugged his papa tight. Then he crouched down and leaned his face against Bianca's soft nose. "Thank you," he whispered. He felt exhausted, and so, so happy to be home.

That night, at the foot of Mount Etna, the ash was still falling,
like strange gray snow. Still, Bianca and the herd slept soundly,
their bellies full of treats. Salvatore, too, was safe in his bed,
fast asleep, thanks to the goats and their special secret senses.

The story of Salvatore and Bianca is inspired by true-life events.

Birds getting restless before a volcanic eruption, snakes waking up from their hibernation ahead of an earthquake, elephants running to the highlands when a tsunami is on the way—like with Salvatore's goats, there are many real-life accounts of animals using a "sixth sense" to protect themselves from impending natural disasters.

Now researchers at the Max Planck Institute of Animal Behavior in Radolfzell, Germany, led by Prof. Dr. Martin Wikelski, are working on a project to make the extraordinary sensory capabilities of many animals useful to humans.

The project is called ICARUS: International Cooperation for Animal Research Using Space.

As part of their research, the ICARUS team fitted goats living around Mount Etna with transmitters on collars and used the data received by the transmitters to compare the animals' movements with volcanic activity.

On January 4, 2012, researchers measured extraordinary activity by the goats.

Six hours later, at 10:20 PM, Mount Etna began spewing large amounts of lava and ash into the air.

Further scientific research was conducted on an Italian farm in the middle of an earthquake-prone region in southern Italy. There, the research team fitted six cows, five sheep, two dogs, two turkeys, two chickens, and a barn rabbit with tools that measure when something starts to move faster and recorded their movements for months. They found that the closer the animals were to the epicenter of an impending earthquake, the sooner they showed unusual behavior. Examples like these strengthen the evidence that animals perceive upcoming catastrophes earlier than humans.

While more research is needed, ICARUS aims to create the conditions to better predict earthquakes, volcanic eruptions, or hurricanes. Understanding the "sixth sense" of animals could help save thousands of lives in the future.

For further information about ICARUS, visit icarus.mpg.de/en.

USCHI MÜLLER has been the coordinator of the ICARUS project at the Max Planck Institute of Animal Behavior in Constance, Germany since 2011. Some of her many various tasks include the planning and implementation of fieldwork missions and animal tagging around the world. She is married and has two daughters. This book is her debut as a children's author.

BRITTANY LANE is a freelance illustrator and fine artist. She formally trained as a biologist and spent over a decade studying fish, plants, and wildlife before pursuing her passion for art. Now she uses visual storytelling as a way to share her love for nature and wildlife with others. She lives with her husband and her dog in Stouffville, Ontario, surrounded by nature.